The Life
of the
Honey Bee

HOPE PAGE

Published in the United States of America

ISBN 978-1-961507-45-6 (SC)

Hope Page Books
222 West 6th Street
Suite 400, San Pedro, CA, 90731
worksofadrianna@gmail.com

Order Information and Rights Permission:

Quantity sales. Special discounts might be available on quantity purchases by corporations, associations, and others. For details, contact the publisher at the address above.

For Book Rights Adaptation and other Rights Permission. Call us at toll-free 1-888-945-8513 or send us an email at admin@stellarliterary.com.

Table of Contents

thought to stop her from driving home that night, Christmas night, Noel's birthday night.

Marian's siblings hated what had become of their baby sister. They hated the hand that life had dealt her that damaged her. Marian was so blessed by God with beauty but cursed by life with tragedy.

As they did all the time when the Maithers came to Detroit, the family gathered at Grammy's house. Noel and Em refused to leave Grammy's house, so Marian attempted to drive home alone. She never made it. Grammy found peace in the fact that it was a one-car accident and no one else was hurt. Cecilia Maithers thought finally her daughter could rest and reunite with her true love.

The night of the funeral, Em tucked Noel into her bed. For such a young girl, Em had lived the life of an adult. Em felt obligated to take care of her little sister. Em hugged Noel and told her, "Everything will be okay!" They both thought that wasn't true, but Em felt like she had to say it. Noel finally fell asleep, and Em went to her own bed.

Noel slept peacefully until something woke her up. She didn't hear a sound, but she felt a good feeling. Bewildered by the unknown, she watched as a stream of light opened and came through her bedroom door. She thought she was dreaming, but she double-checked to ensure she was awake. She could smell her mother's perfume. She could hear her mother say, "Hey! Honey Bee," as her mother often said when she walked into her bedroom. She felt her mother's touch.

With her confused, sleepy eyes, she looked straight into her mother's hazel eyes. Shaken but not afraid, she sat up. Her mother sat next to her on the bed.

"Mommy," she said, but her mother cut her off.

"He gave me time to come to you. I needed to make peace with you and apologize for leaving you how I left you," her mother said. "I'm better now. Heaven has made me better," she added.

"What is heaven like?" Noel asked curiously.

"Just the way you think it is. Just as it sounds," her mommy answered.

"Why did you have to die, Mommy?" Noel asked.

Stroking her daughter's hair and overcome with remorse and regret, "I lost my way a long time ago, and I was nowhere near finding my way back," she answered.

Marian paused. She felt overtaken with emotion. "But don't focus on my life or my death. Think of it as a rebirth, your rebirth. And our love doesn't stop or end here our love was created at the beginning of time and will last beyond the end of time," her mom said with a maturity and clarity she didn't have in life.

"Are you going to stay here with us," Noel asked.

"I was given three nights and three days. That's all. After that, you won't see me again, but I will never be far from you. I will always be with you." she said.

"Why not, Mommy," she asked.

"To give you room to grow and move forward. Seeing me would only block your way by keeping you stuck in pain," she answered. "You are here for your own soul, your own purpose, and to fulfill that you don't need to see me. You only need to feel my love for you," she added.

The two laughed and talked until just before sunrise. Noel rested wrapped in her mother's arm, looking into her mother's glowing, smiling face with her sandy-brown hair flowing as if there was a light breeze blew through the room.

Grammy decided to give the girls an extra week off school. Grammy woke Noel up and led her to the kitchen to eat pancakes. Grammy planned a day of things the girls like to do. Grammy took the girls shopping and to have lunch Downtown.

Everywhere they went that day, everything they did that day, Noel could see her mother smiling and enjoying every moment. Noel felt different about her mother today. Noel could tell her mother was different. Now, her mother was the mommy Noel always wished she had.

On night two after her bath, Noel went to bed eager to talk to her mother. Noel happily snuggled under the covers. Soon, Noel nodded off. She could sense her mother's presence in the room. She could smell her mother's perfume. She sat up, excited to see her mother again They talked about the things they did earlier, which brought up many memories, a few good and some bad.

Just before sunrise, Marian said to her daughter, "Make me a promise."

"What's that, Mommy," Noel asked.

Marian answers, "That you forgive me for my brokenness and misbehavior. I was less than my best self in your presence. I behaved less than a mother in your presence. I thought to satisfy my wants before I thought to fulfill your needs. I am sorry."

Noel collapsed onto Marian's chest.

Marian continues, "I let my brokenness, hurt, pain, and shame keep a stronghold on me, and for that, I am sorry. I was irresponsible, negative, selfish, and dismissive. And if you don't forgive me, that same stronghold will take a grip of you, and you will live a life parallel to mine, making my mistakes. I don't want that for you. If you can forgive me and move on and out of that space, you will have a chance to achieve your greatness."

Still in an embrace, Noel felt peace, calm, and love with her mother unlike ever before. Healing came upon her. Although she didn't know what to call it, she felt her mother hug the hurt away. Her mother held her and rocked her as she fell deeper and deeper asleep.

The next day, Marian spent the day with her mother and two daughters. Grammy and Em could see Noel no longer had a fear or sadness in her eyes. Noel was renewed and refreshed. They couldn't figure out the change; they were just happy to see the change.

The family went to the movies, skating, and dinner at the girls' favorite restaurant. Marian, hidden from Grammy and Em, kept a gentle smile and loving glow on her face. She hoped both her daughters felt her love. She knew too much damage had been done to Em and that her pain ran very deep, but she had high hopes that her girls would be able to move forward in life.

Night came upon the horizon. This night will be their final night together; this will be their final chance to talk. Marian told Noel that Grammy wouldn't be able to take care of the girls for long and that a good family would give the girls a home. She asked Noel to be good to the family because they were good people who really wanted to help and love her and EM.

Marian and Noel talked about Noel's future. Noel asked her mom, "What does a good girl need to do to have a good life?"

Marian told her, "Give yourself time to grow. Get to know yourself and find your passion. Once you figure that out, look to see how you can make the world better by doing whatever it is you love to do. That's what life is all about, making the world better for someone who is in need. Be the best you and live your best life."

Marian added, "Travel! Every chance you get to go somewhere new, go. Study! Try to learn and understand history, culture, and the Bible as much as possible. Live! Make time for yourself to do and appreciate the little things in life. Be open-minded! Be open to receive God. Be adventurous! Try many things and have fun."

Noel listened as the words flowed freely. Marian continued, "You don't have to be like everyone else or do what everyone else is doing. Don't be afraid of your truth. Yes, everyone won't accept your truth, but it is yours and you must be true to and with your truth. Give yourself space to grow, explore, and discover life beyond your borders. Do not stay stuck in any place or situation."

Marian wrapped her arms firmly around Noel as she continued to talk, "And never be afraid to pursue a goal even if it seems like a mighty feat. If you fail, that is only fuel to try it again and do better. When life seems hard or unbearable, remember these three nights and three days. Think of how special you must be for He granted me this time to be with you."

Marian rocked her daughter to sleep for the last time. Marian says, "Remember, Honey Bee, I will never be far from you. I will watch over you every day, praying for you." Those were Marian's last words spoken to her daughter. Although Noel could see her the next day, she could not hear her.

Grammy, Em, and Noel went to see a play at the museum before taking a walk through the festively decorated streets of Downtown Detroit. With the sun diving behind the clouds, Noel watched Marian, outlined with a golden glow, float up in a mystical stream of light all the way beyond the skyline. Marian smiled, blew a kiss, and waved goodbye. Noel felt sad and happy at the same time. Noel knew that Marian was not really gone. Noel had faith that Marian would be with her and, one day, she would be able to see her again.

CHAPTER 2

The Honey Bee's New Hive

Noel nervously sat, clutching her gold necklace with the Honeybee charm at the bus station. Noel was anxious to meet her new family. Em, on the other hand, was miserable in a way that nothing could make her happy.

Em didn't want to go to a new home; she would rather stay with Grammy until the end. In some sense, Em didn't want to be anywhere. She was stuck between a place of nothingness and a place of nowhere. Em knew she loved her grandmother, and she would rather stay with her. One girl sat excited with opportunity for newness, while the other sat sulking in pain and misery waiting for Vernon and Michele Williams.

Before leaving, the girls stood at Grammy's bedside to say goodbye. Grammy had been so weak that no one expected her to be with them much longer. Grammy had Uncle Mike buy Noel a gold necklace with a charm shaped like a honeybee. Grammy gave Em a locket with pictures of mother as a baby and teenager. It was Grammy's way of saying Marian was once good, and, if Em knew her then, Em would have loved her, the good her. But Em didn't love anyone other than Grammy and Noel. Em was already set to not let Vernon and Michele Williams in her heart. The goodbye was tearful and traumatizing for both the girls and Grammy. Grammy didn't want to say goodbye, but she didn't want the girls to watch her die.

Vernon Williams met Michele Maynor on the first day of his junior year in high school. Michele was new in town, and Vernon was impressed the very minute he sat eyes on her. The two had a lot in common: they were both athletes, adopted by good families, and they both were bright. The two became high-school sweethearts and vowed to marry after college and adopt kids when they were established in their careers.

Vernon and Michele's son, Vernon Jr. and daughter, Vanessa, were excited to add to the family. Vernon Jr. (simply called Jr. by his family), twelve, and Vanessa, fourteen, were happy, healthy kids that were grateful to be adopted by such good people. Vernon Jr. was adopted first at age four; Vanessa joined the family two years later. Vernon Jr. and Vanessa both had rough starts in life but felt a great rejuvenation when they were adopted.

One day, an inspired thought moved Michele to add to their family. It was not a coincidence, for Marian had sought out the Williams family. Marian moved upon Michele just when she thought the time was right. From beyond this world, Marian connected with Michele. Marian saw so many similarities between herself and Michele. They had a lot in common in life and in love. They even had a remarkable physical resemblance. Marian fell in love with Michele's heart, and she knew that Michele was the mother she couldn't be.

When Grammy became ill, Maranda Miggins, the child services worker, thought it was time to move Noel and Em. Maranda heard of a couple from Virginia that was looking to adopt. She thought this was the perfect opportunity for Noel and Em to get a new start in a new city.

Em's behavior was becoming disruptive and dangerous. Once Grammy became weak, Em was often kicked out of school for fighting, disrupting the class, or verbally abusing teachers. Em was growing up, and she embodied all the fire that used to be in her mother's eyes when she drank firewater. Em was mad and looking for someone to take it out on.

The entire Williams family came to meet the girls. They were excited and overjoyed to welcome the girls to their family. They greeted the girls with hugs and small gifts. They could sense and see that Noel was a delight. Em, on the other hand, hated them all; not that they did anything to deserve it, but she did, and they could tell immediately. Em hated herself and her life, so she was incapable of loving the Williams family.

The Williams family knew and understood the stress and strain of joining a new family. Mrs. Miggins told them of the girls' history, so they were understanding. They were hopeful to love the walls down that Em built around her heart. They looked forward to Em willingly joining their family.

Michele prepared a big dinner with all the girls' favorite foods. Noel's face glowed with joy the entire night. Em was distant and quiet. The family played games and watched movies, getting to know each other. Although Vernon and Jr. prepared a lovely room for Noel, she opted to sleep with Vanessa. Vanessa read Noel bedtime stories until she fell asleep. Vanessa loved her new sister before midnight.

Em didn't even entertain the thought of joining them. She went to her room. Although Em's room was the room she always dreamed of having, she declined to enjoy it. Her room is pretty much where Em quietly spent the next few weeks alone.

Joseph Monroe was the family counselor assigned to help the Williams family members adjust to the change. Joseph could sense immediately the good, gentle soul of Noel. He knew she would be fine with Mr. and Mrs. Williams. Joseph worried about Em because she refused to give the Williams family a chance. Joseph tried with all his might and intellect to get Em to be happy, but nothing worked.

Noel wished Em would come around, but somehow, she knew it would never happen. Although Noel was sad, she understood why her sister couldn't move forward. Em had experienced the worst possible thing a little girl could experience. Noel knew Em was embarrassed and hurt, so Noel didn't pressure her to change.

Noel felt pure pity for Em. All Noel's life, Marian favored Noel over Em. It was as if Marian hated Em. Noel nor Em could ever figure out why their mother was so cold toward Em. Whatever it was that made Marian hate Em, it ate away at Em's spirit.

Noel enjoyed their new school. Noel made friends fast. Em remained distant and quiet. Her teachers could see the pain on her face. They worried for her because the pain seemed too deep to conquer. Em wore pain like it was an article of clothing; people could see it as if it were her shirt.

Noel flourished with her grades and social life. Although Em didn't say it, she was happy for Noel. Em didn't want Noel to be like her at all. Em found solace in the thought that Noel would be okay with the Williams family. Em felt that they would provide Noel with the life that Noel deserved.

Em penned Noel a goodbye note, listing her hopes and dreams for Noel, and an apology that life together had been so cruel.

Em wrote:

> To My Little Sister, I could not be happy no matter what or where I am because the hurt is too bad to heal or go away. I must leave because my unhappiness will be in your way. I hope you stay safe and protected. I think Mr. and Mrs. Williams will give you a good life, and you will be happy with them. I hope you go to college. I hope you get a good job and take good care of yourself. I hope you will find a good husband and have a happy family. I love you so much.
>
> Em

Em left the note in Noel's locker before she left school to go back to Detroit.

As Noel read the note, she was saddened by the thought of losing her sister. She was relieved that her sister was going to do what she wanted. Noel thought Emelee would be happy going back to Detroit.

Noel showed the note to her teacher who immediately called the principal who then called Michele Williams. The police were called, but there was no sign of Em. Several weeks later, Em turned up at Marian's neighbor's home, Myrna Mills. Myrna took Em to her grandmother's house. Maranda worked it out so that she could stay since everyone knew Em would run away again if sent back to the Williams' home. The Williams family hated to see her go, but they knew she was not happy.

CHAPTER 3

The Rapture of the Honey Bee

That night, Noel fell asleep holding Em's note in her hand. Noel felt lonely and sad because, somehow, she knew she would never live with her sister again. Noel had lost all she had known. She cried herself to sleep, hoping her mother was close.

While asleep, peace fell over Noel. Her body relaxed, and she loosened her grip on the note, and the note fell onto the bed. Noel confusedly stumbled on a strange, unfamiliar place. Noel was walking atop a mountain, through clouds and a calm wind. Noel laid down and looked over the edge. Clouds passed by over her head so closely that she could touch them. She saw the back of a man covered in purple silk over a white linen cloth from head to toe, walking on the trail below her.

The man in purple walked with a golden staff engraved with the word *healing* in his right hand. The man stood taller and bigger than any person Noel had ever seen. His body was totally covered with purple silk, including his face and hands. She saw a jewel-encrusted gold bracelet on his left wrist over the purple silk. The man walked with power and confidence even though his face including his eyes were covered.

Noel sensed the man was not like any other man. A great aura radiated from the man. He suddenly stopped and slowly turned toward Noel. They stared at each other but never spoke or acknowledged each other. Although his face was covered, Noel could see his eyes on her. The man turned and continued to walk until Noel could no longer see him.

Noel, struck with curiosity, got up and walked in the same direction as the man. The sky turned dark. Bigger clouds descended onto the trail of the mountain. Noel walked through the darkness and stepped in the clouds.

Noel frantically looked for the man. Suddenly, Noel's face brushed against another man dressed in purple silk. The contact with the man startled Noel. Noel looked up to see the man's bronze face. His hands and feet were also visible.

The man had thick, long, bushy hair and skin that shined and shimmered like the most expensive polished gold. There was not a flaw to be found in the man. Noel was completely astounded by the man's presence. He smiled at Noel and said, "Young girl, who do you seek?"

"The other man that looks like you," Noel said.

The man replied, "You seek my father! That man is my father, my Lord, and he welcomes you."

"You are Jesus?" Noel asked.

"So, you know my name. If you know my name, you must know my father for he knows you."

Noel reached out to touch the man, totally amazed and speechless.

"Yes, I am real, and it is me," the man said as he reached out to touch Noel's hand.

"Did you come all this way just for me?" Noel asked.

The man smiled and said, "There's no bound I wouldn't or couldn't cross for you." He continued, "For you are one whom he favors, he loves, and I love wholeheartedly."

Noel begins to cry as she listened to the man speak. She said, "Why would he favor me? Am I special?" Noel asked.

The man answered, "No one knows why he [the man pointed up to the man watching from the ledge above] favors who he favors. No one should question why he blesses some and reject others. We all have a path and a purpose we must fulfill. Some paths are harder than others, but they are all ordained in his plan."

The man reached out his hand. "He beckons your presence now. I will carry you," he said. Noel reached out her hand, and the man lifted her into his arms. He cradled her as he effortlessly ascended to the next cliff of the mountain where the man sat. Noel asked, "If your path is tough, does that mean you are cursed, and God doesn't love you?"

The man responded, "You worry about your sister. Don't worry about your sister. Our souls are wise. Our minds and bodies are the ones that are weak. You will see your sister in your father's house, renewed and rejoiced. Your sister's soul is like a lamb to be offered at the altar. Her soul knew its purpose and willingly accepted its duties all for you because she loves you that much."

When they reached the cliff, the bronze-colored man without flaws sat Noel across from the first man completely covered in purple. Next to him laid the staff engraved with *healing* to his right and a golden rod to his left. The man spoke, but he did not move his mouth. Noel could hear his voice in her mind. "You are cold," he said. A fire appeared between the two of them.

"You are God, and that man is your son, Jesus," Noel said.

"So, you know me," the man responded.

"My grandmother told me all about you," Noel said.

The man was pleased. Noel could see him although he was covered in purple silk. He smiled at the little girl and said, "Honey Bee, you are loved in heaven. You have been blessed with a gift." He handed her the staff from his right. When the staff touched her hand, light radiated from the word *healing*. Noel looked at the staff and the light.

"Your destiny and gifts were planned at the beginning of time. Don't let the tragedy and trauma divert you from your path. Your mother and father are cheering you on," the man said.

Noel said humbly, "But what about my sister? Is she cursed? She suffers so much!"

The man got up and began to walk away joined by the younger man. "Don't worry about your sister. She loves you. She is selfless and courageous. She is a willing soldier in this war. A seat awaits her in my house, and it won't be long before she lives in love with me and my son."

Noel yelled, "Will I see either of you again," as the men walked away.

The younger man said, "Young girl, we are with you all the time. We see you all day, each day. More importantly, you will feel us all around you every day." The two men ascended beyond the night sky, and Noel watched until she could no longer see them.

Noel woke up feeling as though the dream was more than a dream. It was as if God was telling her that her sister would be saved and okay. She also thought God was telling her that her life's purpose is to be a doctor.

CHAPTER 4

How the Honey Bee Came to Be

Luverne, Crenshaw County, Alabama, "the Friendliest City in the South" welcomed a beautiful baby girl, Marian Suzette Maithers. Marian was the youngest of the twelve Maithers children. Marian was named after her grandmothers, Mary Ann Saunders, and Suzette Mary Lee Maithers.

Marian was the mirror image of her mother, Cecilia Maithers, with hazel eyes and a head full of soft sandy-brown hair. Cecilia was a devout Baptist church member who married Charles Maithers when she was sixteen years old.

Cecilia gave birth to her first child, Charles Maithers Jr., when she was eighteen years old. Seven boys and four girls followed Junior: Michael Maithers, Xavier Maithers, Anese Maithers, May Belle Maithers, James Daniel Maithers, Paul John Maithers, Covelle Lee Maithers, Anna May Maithers, Arlan Maithers, and David Maithers.

Cecilia had been a good mother to her kids over the years. They did not have much but they were happy. Cecilia was full of faith and holiness, and she worked to instill that in her children. Cecilia and her kids never missed a Sunday service or Bible study class. Charles worked a steady stream of jobs to support their growing family. There weren't many means to provide for such a big family in such a small town during the Jim Crow South era. Charles would travel the south, looking for work over the years, leaving Cecilia alone with the kids.

Cecilia didn't mind much because she saw Charles as a good man, a good provider. Cecilia and Charles both came from good, stable Christian homes, and they wanted to provide the same for their children. Cecilia saw things as if they were both doing their part to achieve their common goal.

On this day, her thirty-eighth birthday, Cecilia Maithers welcomed her last child with her husband and her children surrounding her. There was something about this baby they all loved. She was blessed with beauty just like her mother.

There was nostalgia because she was the final piece to make the family whole. The older children had left the nest to begin their adult life. Junior, Michael, and Xavier all joined the armed forces the day after their high school graduation. They thought joining the service was the best way to escape a small town and a life of poverty. Anise moved to North Carolina to attend college where she received a full scholarship.

With the four oldest children gone, the house seemed a tad bit bigger, but Marian and the other seven siblings kept the house full of noise and movement. Marian was doted on by all her siblings. They kept her smiling and entertained her.

One day, when Marian was about six months old, a typical day in the Maithers' household with the kids at school and Cecilia taking care of the house and Marian, a knock at the door startled Cecilia. It was Reverend Sutton. Cecilia shocked by his presence said, "Hi, Reverend, I hadn't expected to see you."

The Reverend slightly bowed his head, spoke in a serious tone, "I have come to deliver bad news." He paused to take a deep breath. "I hate to tell you this, Sister Maithers, but Brother Charles was in a…a…a [he stuttered with grief] car accident with Deacon Stanley and Gerald just outside the county line, they're all gone [his voice broke]."

Cecilia fell to the floor screaming with grief. Reverend Sutton tried to comfort her. Stan and Gerald were his brothers, so he knew firsthand the misery and despair she felt. Reverend Sutton sat with Cecilia in his arms, rocking to comfort them both.

Cecilia was totally blindsided by Charles' death. This is something she did not expect to happen. Both she and Charles were too young for one to die. Reverend Sutton helped Cecilia to the couch. Members of the church started to arrive and gather in the house. They took over her house duties and immediately started tending to the baby, while Reverend explained more about the car accident that took three young men's lives.

Cecilia could see and hear Reverend speaking, but she didn't comprehend. She was stuck in the initial shock. She couldn't grasp the fact she would never see her husband again.

The funerals for Brother Charles, Deacon Stanley Sutton, and Gerald Sutton were hard for the whole congregation. Three wives were left alone to care for their children. Reverend Sutton did what he could to hide the pain of losing two brothers to console the grieving wives and children. Cecilia trudged through her pain to remain strong for her children.

With four children gone, Marian still had eight children to provide for and get through school. The church congregation donated as much as they could to the three families. In one instance, twenty-one children were left without a father. The deaths were devastating for the First Baptist Congregation.

Cecilia's face never really had a sign of light or happiness after Charles' death. She tried to show the kids love, but the pain of losing Charles killed a piece of her soul. She thought she'd die because it hurt so much. Every night she cried herself to sleep. The kids tried to pretend they didn't hear her. They did what they could to comfort and help her.

After a few months, the family fell into a routine. Cecilia worked two jobs, and the kids supported and cared for each other. They took turns cooking, cleaning, and babysitting Marian. Not one of the children complained because they were proud of how their mother survived and pulled through losing her true love. In time, life became bearable. They were able to laugh and smile again.

Eight summers passed, and Cecilia's oldest kids were gone. Cecilia and Marian were left alone. They were happy, and times had become easier with just two mouths to feed. Marian went to school while Cecilia worked. Marian always arrived home first. Marian walked home with her friends, so Cecilia didn't worry much. The neighbors would keep an eye on her until Cecilia arrived home. One day, eight-year-old Marian didn't arrive home as scheduled, so one of her neighbors, Brother Jeff Gentry, went looking for her. Mrs. Gentry called Cecilia at work because Mrs. Gentry had an eerie feeling something wasn't right. Mrs. Gentry went to every neighbor to spread the word. The neighbors formed a search party. The people of Luverne always did what they could to look out for their own.

The closer to night fall, the more the neighbors panicked. Just after the sun set, Brother Gentry and Brother Waylen found Marian beaten, bloody, and unconscious behind a small building.

In Marian's unconsciousness, she dreamt of running in the sun through a field of daisies until she was snatched by a man. Just as the man grabbed her in the dream, Brother Gentry picked her up. Marian screamed.

Brother Gentry's knees were weak as he carried the limp body of the broken little girl. Both of her eyes were swollen shut. Her legs were completely covered in blood. Her left arm seemed broken. Dried blood filled both her ears and covered her lips.

Brother Gentry eyes flooded with tears. Brother Waylen helped put Marian in the backseat. They drove her to the hospital because they didn't want Cecilia to see Marian in such a battered and disgraced state.

Brother Waylen left Brother Gentry at the hospital to rush to get Cecilia. When Brother Waylen arrived at the hospital with Cecilia, Marian was telling the police how three teenaged white boys took her as she was about to turn the corner to go home from school. She never seen the three boys before, so she had no idea why they chose her.

The sheriff didn't seem very interested in the story, but the deputy seemed heartbroken and sympathetic to Marian and Cecilia. The deputy talked to Brother Gentry and Brother Waylen with respect and concern. They explained the little girl had no dad because he died when she was just a baby, which made the deputy more empathetic.

The doctors and nurses took good care of Marian in the hospital because they knew she wouldn't receive justice in the system. She stayed in the hospital for three days, but there was nothing more the doctors could do. The true damage that was done couldn't be repaired by medical means. The physical damage that was done to her face and body would heal, but the damage to her soul and mind may never.

The doctors told Cecilia only time could tell if her reproductive system would function properly. It was hard to predict if she would be able to bear children as an adult.

Before the rape and beating, Marian was a happy girl blessed by God with beauty and a gorgeous smile that was on display most of every day of her life. After the rape, Marian became shy, ashamed, and a selective mute. Truth be told, no one really expected anything different from her. Everyone thought it would be impossible to recover from something so brutal.

The deputy, Deputy William Hurt, saw Brother Gentry one day and stopped to talk to him about the three boys that hurt Marian. Deputy Hurt told Brother Gentry that there's no need to fear the boys. The three boys, Robert "Bobby" Blake, Matthew Walters, and Ken Newman were three boys of Mountain Brook in Southeastern Jefferson County, Alabama.

The boys were drunk teenagers passing through and looking for trouble. The parents agreed to send them to military school when they heard of the rape. Deputy Hurt handed Brother Gentry a brown bag with $10,000 in it. He said, "The families of the boys sent it to help the little girl with medical expenses." The truth is, they only sent $8,000, but Deputy Hurt added $2,000 of his own money. It was his entire life savings from his bank account.

The deputy asked Brother Gentry to keep this quiet because he would receive repercussions for talking to the boys' parents. Deputy Hurt had been specifically warned by Sheriff Boyd not to investigate the matter further. Once the sheriff received word that the perpetrators were the rich boys, he was intent on not ruffling the parent's feathers.

Brother Gentry took Marian and Cecilia to the bus station. He never told anyone, not even his wife, of the conversation he had with Deputy Hurt. The thought of the boys getting away with hurting Marian and the parents sending money sickened his soul. He knew Cecilia could use the $10,000 to start over in Detroit. He knew if she knew where the money came from, she would not take it. When he walked them to the bus, Brother Gentry handed Cecilia a satchel filled with the $10,000.

Brother Gentry explained that the neighbors had taken up a collection for the girl. Cecilia's mouth dropped when she saw the amount of money. She refused to accept it. "It is just too much. I can't take that."

Brother Gentry refused to take it back. He pushed them on the bus. "Go now! Take care of that little girl! Make sure she has a good life!" Cecilia broke down with tears at the thought of the tragedy and the generosity of her neighbors.

Cecilia and Marian boarded the bus to Detroit, never to return to Luverne. Moving from a small southern city to a big northern urban city in the 1960's called for a big adjustment for Marian and Cecilia. They had to adapt to the ways of the fast-paced city. As promised, Shelby Ann arranged for Cecilia to get a job at the plant on Detroit's east side. With the $10,000 in the bank and a hearty weekly income, Cecilia quickly bought a nice house and a brand-new car.

Although they had a few relatives in Detroit, Marian and Cecilia spent most of their time alone. With the ravage they suffered back home, neither Marian nor Cecilia felt much like social interaction. They got into the routine of school for Marian and work for Cecilia. In their free time, they had mother-daughter time, going to the movies, shopping Downtown, and eating nice meals together.

Marian did well in school in Detroit. Although she remained quiet and shy, she got good grades and had a pleasant personality. Her teachers adored her and doted on her manners and work ethics.

Cecilia loved working on the line at the plant. She was one of the few women who worked at the plant. She did her job and did it well, so she had earned the respect and love of her coworkers. Cecilia worked six days per week, even worked overtime whenever she could. Cecilia never missed a day or left work early. Marian never missed a day of school and never got less than a B+ on any assignment.

It seemed so quick, but the years passed, and Marian was a senior in high school. Marian had blossomed into a beautiful young woman. She worked and trained hard every day. Sports was an escape from her reality. Marian had become a good athlete, playing tennis, and running track. Marian was learning to smile again.

Working so hard for so long, Cecilia was able to save quite a bit of money. Additionally, Marian received several scholarships to cover her classes and books for all four years. As she did all through high school, Marian excelled in college in both sports and academics.

One fall day of her junior year, Mokeith Jenkins, the star quarterback at the university Marian attended, asked the shy and sheltered Marian out on a date. She hesitated, but he convinced her that it would be innocent fun.

That night, Mokeith took Marian for a burger and milkshake then to a drive-in movie. All went well and was innocent fun for Marian. Mokeith parked in an isolated area a few miles from the dorms. They had a friendly conversation for a while, but when Marian asked to go back to her dorm, Mokeith's demeanor changed. He grabbed Marian's arm then her hair to push her to the backseat of the car where he beat and took advantage of her. Mokeith became a monster right before her eyes.

Mokeith stopped hurting Marian to fix his clothes. He got back in the front seat to drive to the main road. Marian tried to fix her clothes as she silently sobbed in the back seat. Mokeith got out of the car, yanked open the back door, and began mercilessly beating Marian in the face and head. It was as if he punished her for making him hurt her.

He pulled her out of the car by her beautiful hair and threw her on the side of the road like he was discarding trash. He quickly pulled off, leaving Marian on the side of the road just as she had been left when she was hurt the first time.

Cecilia sat watching late-night television alone in her home when the phone rang. A man driving down the road found Marian lying on the side of the road. Cecilia could have died; in fact, a piece of her soul died the day Charles died, a little more the night of the first attack, and tonight, her soul died completely. Cecilia was living on empty from the moment she hung up the phone.

Cecilia drove with tears flowing from her eyes until she reached the hospital. She was beyond devastated and speechless. Cecilia wanted to get to her daughter's side and console her, hold her, and love her.

When Cecilia walked into the emergency room, Dr. Avery assured her that Marian would survive and there was no permanent physical damage. However, Dr. Avery warned Cecilia that Marian had suffered a severe, savage beating to the face. He asked her to brace herself before walking in the room.

Unable to hold her emotions together, Cecilia took one look at Marian and fainted. Cecilia's entire body suffered paralysis as she blacked out and hit the floor. The ER staff rushed to her side to check on her. The nurses rushed to lift her off the floor and into a wheelchair.

Marian cried listening to the shuffle of the nurses rush to Cecilia. When Cecilia finally made it to Marian's side; she said sobbing, "Baby, I'm so sorry this happened to you!" The two embraced and cried.

The police came to talk to Cecilia. They sat her down to explain what had happened thus far in the case. They had the young man in custody. Although Mokeith swore to the police he dropped her off right after the movie and went straight to his dorm room, the police held him in custody. Several people reported seeing his car parked on the road during the time of the attack.

Since the assault didn't happen on campus, the local police were able to control the investigation. The detective, Mike Brown, explained Mokeith Jenkins had been named in three on-campus assaults, but the university was able to cover those up because he was profitable on the football field.

Marian refused to go back to school and begged to go home with her mother. Dr. Avery asked Marian to follow up with him in a few weeks. Cecilia took Marian home to care for her. They both were devastated and overcome with grief. The next few weeks were filled with silence, crying, and stillness. Marian stayed in her room under the cover. She barely ate or slept. Cecilia worried about Marian and tried to convince her to eat. Cecilia didn't know what to do but call on God, pray, and ask for grace and mercy.

Cecilia took Marian to follow up with Dr. Avery. Dr. Avery could see that Marian was in a deep depression, so it burdened him to tell her she was pregnant. Marian fell to the floor with violent tremors. She immediately lost touch with reality. Dr. Avery sent her for a psychiatric evaluation. She stayed in the psychiatric hospital for the entire pregnancy. Doctors feared Marian would harm herself if left unsupervised.

Cecilia knew this was the breaking point of her daughter. She couldn't even think of what they would do with the baby. How would her daughter cope with a daily reminder of being brutally violated for a second time? Cecilia prayed and left the situation for God to manage.

The doctors at the psychiatric hospital talked to Cecilia about adoption and how both families could benefit. Cecilia didn't know whether they should keep or give up the baby; she thought the decision was best addressed by Marian.

Marian successfully carried the baby full term and began to come around. During one of Cecilia's Saturday visits, Marian's water broke, and she went into labor. After twelve hours of intense labor pains, Marian gave birth to Emelee Amil Maithers. For some reason, Marian refused to give up her baby. Although it pained her to look at Emelee, she thought it was best to raise her own child.

When Emelee was three months old, Marian finally came home to be with her mother and baby. Marian opted to finish her education at the newly founded university within the city limits.

Em was a good baby. She didn't cry much. Cecilia and Marian were working together to care for and provide for Em. Cecilia thought things were looking up and this too would pass.

Surprisingly, Marian was making friends and doing well at the university. She was even being an attentive mother to Em. Marian was making the best of the situation; she was relieved after the perpetrator of the hideous crime went to jail. Marian didn't have to go to court to face Mokeith. With Marian's gentle mental-health state, prosecutors thought it was best to quietly work out a deal with Mokeith.

While on campus, Marian caught the eye of Everett Stephens, a very handsome, intelligent medical student studying to be a pediatric surgeon. Marian fell completely head over heels for him. She told him all about Alabama and how she became pregnant with Em. Hearing of her past struggles only made Everett love Marian more.

When the relationship got serious, Everett became a devoted father to Em. Everett truly believed every child needed a devoted father. Marian told Everett she was pregnant after Em's second birthday. Everett asked Marian to marry him, so they live as husband and wife with their two kids.

On a pretty spring day, the hopeful couple went down to city hall and were married. Everett purchased a house not too far from Cecilia's so she could help with the kids. Cecilia was pleased how life was working out for her daughter.

Everett, Marian, and Em went out to enjoy a family fun night of pizza, popcorn, and a movie on a December night. At the end of their family night, they walked through the parking lot, laughing and beaming with a bright glow of happiness. Just as Everett buckled Em in her car seat, a masked man with a gun approached Everett from behind. He stuck the gun in Everett's back and yelled, "Give me the keys!" Marian, buckled in the passenger seat, screamed. Everett turned toward the man, but before he could speak, the masked man shot him twice in the chest.

Marian rushed to Everett who had fallen onto Em in her car seat. Blood covered him and, a crying, Em. The masked assailant ran away and off into the night. Everett grabbed for Marian as he gasped for air. Everett began to choke as death filled his eyes. Everett gasped three more times before letting his grip go of both Marian's hand and his life.

Soon, the parking lot was filled with police and emergency workers. Marian went into shock, hyperventilating and crying uncontrollably, so the emergency workers took her and Em to the hospital. Another late-night call came for Cecilia to come to the hospital and see about Marian and pick up Em. Cecilia arrived at the emergency room panicked and devastated.

The police released custody of Em to Cecilia, and Dr. Hausenberg warned her that Marian was in a fragile state. Cecilia told Dr. Hausenberg about the Alabama incident and the conception of Emelee. Dr. Hausenberg became extremely concerned based on the history of Marian's mental health, so he sent her to an emergency psychiatric facility.

By the time Cecilia was allowed to see Marian, Marian was a human zombie. She did not speak, eat, move, or respond to anyone or anything for days. Marian couldn't even make it to Everett's homegoing in Georgia. Cecilia and Em went to say goodbye to the only father Em had known. Everett in his casket reminded Cecilia of Charles in his casket. It took all of Cecilia's strength to not break down at Everett's funeral. Cecilia was at the point where she didn't think she could survive another tragedy.

Very early Christmas morning, Marian gave birth to Noel Ann Marie Stephens. Noel was born blessed by God's grace just like her mother, with hazel eyes and soft sandy-brown hair. Marian looked just like Cecilia's baby photo at birth, and Noel looked just like Marian's baby photo.

It is possible that the love between her mother and father blessed Noel. There's a possibility that her parents sacrificed their lives for hers, or the repeated tragedies in her mother's life took the brunt of any burden Noel was destined to face. All in all, Noel was destined to have a good life despite the tragedies her mother faced.

Marian spent six months in the psychiatric hospital. When she was released, she was prescribed several medications. Cecilia took care of the girls while Marian tried to work things out in her mind. She never recovered.

Marian became addicted to the medications. Marian's soul died that night with Everett. She was empty and drugs gave her the fuel to self-destruct. Marian began to display dangerous, reckless behavior that would slowly kill her.

To soothe her pain, Marian overused alcohol. It wasn't that Marian liked or wanted alcohol; she needed something unknown to herself, and alcohol was readily accessible.

Marian was so caught in her addiction to alcohol that she couldn't care for her daughters. Marian became Cecilia's babysitter, and the girls hated every moment they had to spend with Marian. Cecilia was stricken with grief because she didn't know what to do for her baby girl, so she settled in the routine of fulfilling the duties of her daughter.

Cecilia accepted that the pressure of the attacks and the murder of the only man she loved had pushed her daughter beyond her breaking point. Cecilia, completely empty herself, was functioning but not living. Two dead women were raising two little girls. One of the women was havoc and chaos to the girls, while the other woman represented peace and safety to the girls.

Although Marian was spiteful toward everyone and disconnected from the world, she saw something special in Noel. Although Marian couldn't articulate it, Marian favored Noel because Noel was conceived in love. She always took the time to acknowledge Noel's presence, but Em could've died each time she walked into a room with her mother because Marian never acknowledged Em's presence.

Em noticed early in life how her mother's face would soften, and her voice would lighten for Noel, but Marian's face remained blank whenever she saw Em and she rarely spoke to Em. Marian loved Noel just enough that Noel didn't feel as abandoned and hopeless as Em.

Marian never told Em any of the things that mothers tell their daughters such as "I love you," "you're beautiful," or "you're special." Em didn't understand why her mother behaved the way she did or why she needed to be inebriated all the time. The tension between Marian and Em raged like a wildfire that was bound to scorch the earth.

Cecilia decided to retire from the plant to spend more time with her granddaughters. Cecilia made sure the girls ate, had nice, clean clothes, and had a safe place to sleep. Cecilia took them to school and picked them up. Cecilia helped them with their homework. She went to all their school functions. Cecilia didn't want to incite confrontation with Marian, so she didn't try to take full custody of the girls. Most days the girls refused to go home with Marian. When Marian wasn't in the mood to argue with the girls, she let them have their way.

Cecilia was overwhelmed with her daughter's decisions and lifestyle. She was perplexed by the current circumstances, but she was hoping for a brighter future. Cecilia arranged for the girls to get counseling. She figured the situation was best navigated by a professional.

CHAPTER 5

What Became of Emelee Amil Maithers

After Em went back to Detroit, she lived with Grammy. Em became Grammy's caretaker.

In their time alone, Em and Grammy had a deep, open, and honest conversation. Em told Grammy the things Grammy didn't know, like how Howard and Walter hurt her. Em told Grammy how Howard and Walter violated her while her mother was drunk.

Her mother was so drunk that she passed out. After the men had their way with Marian while she was unconscious, they came into Em's room to have their way with her tiny body. Em explained to Grammy that she didn't tell Marian about Howard because she didn't know what to say. Em said, "When I told her about Walter hurting me, she smacked me and ignored me."

Grammy was speechless. She cried with heartbreak. She couldn't believe what Em had been through or that Marian sat by while her daughter experienced the same torment she suffered. Grammy cried and cried holding Em in a tight embrace.

Grammy received the last blow her soul could take. Grammy couldn't understand why Marian and Emelee had been so cursed. What was it that made them destined for a life of hell on Earth? Grammy cried out to the Lord for mercy, mercy for Em and mercy for Marian.

With a heavy heart, Cecilia revealed the whole truth about Marian's life. Cecilia thought Em needed to know what made her mother behave as she did. Cecilia told Em about the day Marian was kidnapped and violated as a child, the truth about her real father, the two stays in a mental hospital, and the death of Everett. Em cried because she was hurt for her mother. Em cried because she was hurt for herself.

Three days after that night, Cecilia went to sleep and didn't wake up.

Em was left alone just when she was feeling as though she could come out of her misery. The Maithers kids came to Detroit to bury their mother right next to Marian. This was a hard time for them because they loved and adored their mother.

The Williams family came to Detroit with Noel to attend the funeral. When Em and Noel saw each other, they ran to each other and embraced. They held each other for a long time. Noel and Em walked to the casket hand in hand and stood looking at the one woman that had brought them solace during the rough years.

Cecilia had been a good woman her whole life. She made no enemies, and she was good to her children and grandchildren. The funeral was tough for them all. They were sad to say goodbye, but they were relieved that she wouldn't suffer anymore. Cecilia's oldest son Charles Jr. said during the funeral, "My mother fought a good fight, and I know my father was there at the pearly gates to welcome her with open arms."

Three days after the funeral, the Maithers children began returning to their homes, leaving Emelee all alone again. Mr. and Mrs. Williams invited her to come back to Virginia, but she opted to stay in Detroit. Emelee Amil Maithers had no place to go, no home, no family, and no parents. This began her life of place-to-place living.

Em's first stop was staying with Myrna. Myrna's house was the party house. One could find plenty of firewater any time of the day, any day of the week, but one couldn't find food, love, or supervision. Em existed at Myrna's house. She was just grateful every day she made it through without being touched or hit. Living with Myrna was much like living with Marian; no one cared if she lived or died.

When Myrna was evicted for not paying the rent, Em had nowhere to go but to Shelby Ann's daughter's house. She didn't know anyone else in Detroit, and she refused to go stay with her relatives out of town. Shelby Ann and her daughter, Abigail, shared a home, near the plant that Shelby Ann and Cecilia retired from after decades of working.

Abigail had four children and supported them with state assistance. Bringing Em into their home would mean more food stamps and a bigger check for Abigail, so she was more than willing to take her into their home. Abigail had no intention of taking care of Em or loving her.

The best thing about living with Shelby Ann and Abigail was the fact that Em ate three meals a day. She didn't get much love or attention, but she was grateful for a quiet, clean place to lay her head and to eat three meals a day. Em went to school because it was a requirement to live with Abigail and Shelby Ann.

Em and Noel wrote to each other every week, but Em refused to call or see her. Em didn't want to interrupt Noel's life. Em wanted Noel to live a life unburdened by their past, so Em never brought up the past. Em was happy to hear about the positive things in Noel's life. Em was grateful to Mr. and Mrs. Williams for giving Noel a chance to live a good life.

One day, on her way to school, a car pulled alongside Em. The driver was Ray-Won, which was short for Raymond Wontor. Ray-Won was a street hustler that specialized in shooting dice, selling drugs, and manipulating women. Em didn't realize how dangerous it was to begin a relationship with Ray.

Em began sneaking out of the house and skipping school to be with him. In her mind, Em had finally found someone to love her. It wasn't hard for Ray to convince Em to run away from home to live with him. Em thought she was running away to be in a relationship with Ray. Em had no idea what was in store for her.

Emelee had grown into a beautiful, young woman with light-brown eyes and long, dark hair. Em felt so happy with Ray-Won. He bought her nice, expensive clothes and jewelry. He dropped her off and picked her up from school. She loved that everyone knew she was with Ray-Won. People knew Ray-Won was too old to have a relationship with Em, but no one dared say anything.

In the two months that she and Ray had been living together, Shelby Ann or Abigail never came looking for her. On one hand, Em felt worthless because her family didn't come looking for her. On the other hand, Em felt proud and happy because she was with Ray. Em had officially become a woman on her own at least in her mind.

When Em came home from school, Ray had two strange men in the apartment consuming firewater and drugs. Em had never seen the men before. Ray told her the men were his friends. Em immediately felt uncomfortable. She went searching for food, but there was none. She went to the bedroom looking for her money, but it was gone. Em settled in the bedroom to do her homework despite the unsettling feelings she had.

Em could hear and smell the men smoking and drinking, filling the apartment with the smell of devastation. Em had an eerie feeling that something bad was about to happen. The smell in the air made memories of Em's childhood flood her mind. The hunger pangs and sounds she heard made her feel just like she did when she lived with her mother. Em had grown to rely on Ray because he fed her every day, he kept her in a clean apartment, he bought her food and clothes, and he made her feel loved.

The apartment suddenly became unnervingly quiet just before Ray came bursting into the bedroom drunk off firewater and high from his own supply of drugs. He stood looking at Em. Starving and frightened, she asked for money to go get food. He smiled before he said, "People have to work for money." He waved at his friends to invite them into the room.

Em was shocked, confused, and speechless. She could not move even though her mind screamed run. Ray said, "You're hungry right! We are too. You feed us, and we'll feed you. That's a fair trade!" Tears streamed down Em's face.

Ray's betrayal completely broke Em's heart again. She felt just like that little girl her mother smacked to the floor the night she told her that Walter had hurt her. She quickly tried to leave the room, but Ray caught her and threw her on the bed.

For hours, the three men took turns brutalizing Em. When they were done, Ray pushed her off the bed and told her to put on her clothes and get all her stuff. He said laughing, "You got to go!"

Em said, "I have nowhere to go!"

Ray laughed and said, "You can't stay here."

Ray and his friends took Em to a big house. They gave her some money and pushed her out of the car. Ray said, "Go up there to see Ms. Minnie. She'll take care of you!" Em, lost, broken, and abandoned again, walked toward the door crying and ashamed.

As she walked up the stairs, she realized Ray was just like the men who had hurt her as a child. Em was exhausted and hungry as she walked towards the door. She reluctantly knocked on the door, but she knew she had nowhere else to go.

Ms. Minnie opened the door and saw Em's blank and empty face. Instantly, Ms. Minnie grew empathy for Em. Ms. Minnie recognized herself in Em: pain, loneliness, used, and abused. Ms. Minnie said, "Come on in here, Girl!" Em did not speak or look up. Ms. Minnie said, "Let me fix you something to eat." Em carried a garbage bag full of the things she once thought were prized possessions (because Ray gave them to her).

As Ms. Minnie cooked, she made small talk with Em. She asked, "What's your name?" Em told her that her name was Emelee. Ms. Minnie said, "You're such a beautiful young lady, but you look to young to be messing with Ray." Ms. Minnie gave Em food. "When you're done, I'll run you a bath and take you to your room." Ms. Minnie watched Em eat, and she thought about her own story.

Ms. Minnie came to Detroit as a young girl. She dropped out of high school to run the streets with her older best friend. Ms. Minnie went from being an innocent high-school student to a drug-addicted girl working the streets of Detroit. Now she runs a house for Ray. She takes care of Ray's girl, making sure they get food, clothing, medical care, and help them prepare for dates.

Ms. Minnie was usually cold and distant to the girls Ray brought to the house, but there was something different about Em that melted Ms. Minnie's heart. Ms. Minnie was the first person to truly love Em other than her grandmother and Noel.

After a few days, Em was also getting to know the other six girls in the house. Em found out that Ray-Won had done the exact same thing to every girl in the house. The other girls told Em the details of how Ray manipulated them. Ray saw a vulnerable, beautiful girl that he could easily manipulate.

Em realized she had been too vulnerable, which made her a target for predatory men. Em was hurt and ashamed of her own vulnerability. Em was mad at herself for thinking Ray would love her.

Ms. Minnie took extra good care of Em. Mrs. Minnie made sure Em went to school every day, Em ate three meals a day, and Em had the best dates. Ms. Minnie didn't want Em to live this life, but she knew Ray would kill them both if Em didn't bring in money. Em never spoke to Ray again. Ms. Minnie was the go-between for Ray and the girls. When the girls refused to listen to Ms. Minnie, Ray sent men to the house to beat the defiant girls.

Em was again hating her life. She went to school in the day and hustled for Ray at night. Em wanted a way out, but she knew Ray wouldn't let her go. Ms. Minnie became like a mom to Em. Ms. Minnie convinced Em to write a letter to her father who was now out of prison and rebuilding his life as a free man. Mokeith wrote Em back, and the two agreed to meet.

One night, Em refused to go on a date, so Ray sent some guys over to the house to beat Em. They smacked her around until her eye was swollen and black and her lip was bloodied. Em was hesitant to meet her dad with a bruised face, but she was curious.

Ms. Minnie drove Em to meet Mokeith at a restaurant. It was awkward, but the two began to talk about his life before and after jail and Em's childhood. Mokeith felt bad that his daughter had such a rough time in life. In Mokeith's mind, the sins of the father had damned the daughter to a life of hell. Mokeith apologized to Em for his behavior toward her mother.

Before leaving the restaurant, Mokeith asked Em about her face. Em reluctantly told Mokeith of her situation with Ray-Won. Em didn't expect him to do anything, but it felt good to share her burden with someone else. Mokeith and Em kept in touch after that meeting. He called to check on her often, and every now and then, they met in person. One night, Mokeith called Em, and she was crying. Em told him she wanted out of this life, but she feared Ray.

Mokeith researched Ray-Won. Mokeith found out where he hung out, where he did business, and who he hung with most of the time. Mokeith began following Ray and learned his scheduled. Ray had a wife and kids: three girls and two boys. Ray lived in a big house and had nice cars. Em and the girls never knew he had a wife and kids. When Mokeith told Em about Ray's wife and children, it was another smack in the face.

Mokeith had enough of Ray abusing his daughter, so he followed Ray home to make his move. Ray was extremely drunk. Mokeith walked up to Ray as he got out the car in his driveway. Ray never saw him coming. Ray thought his real life was a secret from the streets. Ray never even looked around to see if anyone was nearby.

Mokeith put five bullets in Ray's head with a 9mm equipped with a silencer. Mokeith walked away unseen by anyone. After sunrise, Ray's wife saw his body leaning in the driver's seat. She walked up to the car and saw blood and brain matter all over the car and ground.

The word began to spread in the streets about Raymond Wontor's death. When Em and the girls caught heed of the word, they were relieved. They didn't have a future, but they didn't have their past. The girls had been freed. Mokeith called Em to meet him. Mokeith gave Em a bag of money, a bag of money he took from Ray-Won's car.

Mokeith told Em, "Go! Get out of here! Today! Never come back to Detroit." Em hugged Mokeith. In that moment, she was relieved that he was her dad. Mokeith told her, "You call me! Let me know where you are and what's going on! I am here whenever you need me! Now go!"

Em ran off in excitement. With Ray-Won gone, the girls were free. Em, Ms. Minnie, and two of the girls decided to go to Chicago where they could have a fresh start. The rest of the girls decided to stay in Detroit.

The group of women said goodbye to each other at the train station in Downtown Detroit. The goodbye was the saddest and happiest moment they spent together. They knew they would never see each other again, but they were glad they were freed from their life as Ray's slaves.

Em, Ms. Minnie, Keinosha, and Amina moved to the bustling south side of Chicago. They were nervous to be in a new place but excited at a chance for a new life. With the money Mokeith gave Em, she was able to get a nice apartment and cars for Miss Minnie and herself.

The one funny thing about a new life is an old problem: the need for money. Amina and Keinosha quickly found working nine to five wasn't enough for them. Em and Ms. Minnie tried to convince them to stay away from the street life. Amina and Keinosha left Em and Ms. Minnie to move back to Detroit.

Em got her GED, a job, and went to school at night to study nursing. Ms. Minnie was a server at a restaurant during the day. The two lived as mother and daughter. Ms. Minnie cared for Em as if Em was her own daughter. Em was happy again. She had peace living with Ms. Minnie. Em was looking to the future full of hope.

Ms. Minnie always got home first and cooked for Em and made sure the apartment was clean. One ordinary night, Ms. Minnie sat waiting for Em. It was well past Em's usual arrival time. Ms. Minnie worried, staring out the window. She had a strange feeling something was wrong.

Ms. Minnie paced the floor for hours while she called everywhere she could think of to look for Em. Em hadn't dated anyone since arriving in Chicago, so there was no man in her life. Em wouldn't be late without calling Ms. Minnie.

Ms. Minnie fell asleep holding the phone. There was a knock at the door. Ms. Minnie was awakened with confusion and fear. Em had a key, so Ms. Minnie couldn't comprehend why she would knock. Ms. Minnie thought she lost her key as she rushed to the door.

It was two men dressed in suits. They introduced themselves as Detective Sams and Detective Harford. They asked her name, and she told them she was Minnie Wells. She asked, "What's going on?"

Detective Sams asked, "Does Emelee Maithers live at this address?"

Ms. Minnie said, "Yes! We moved here together from Detroit."

Detective Harford asked, "Are you two relatives?"

Ms. Minnie answered, "No! Not by blood. She's like my adopted daughter."

Detective Harford asked, "Does she have relatives you can contact?"

Ms. Minnie answered, "She has a father in Detroit, but they're not that close. She also has a sister she writes, but she doesn't talk much about her. What is going on? Is there something wrong with Emelee?"

Detective Sams said, "We are sorry to inform you that Ms. Maithers was found dead this evening. We need you to come down and identify the body." Ms. Minnie broke down with grief. She fell to her knees crying. The detectives helped her up and over to the couch.

Ms. Minnie sobbed. "What happened to Emelee?"

Detective Harford said, "She was murdered." Ms. Minnie cried out with sorrow of a broken heart.

Detective Sams asked Ms. Minnie to get any contact information for Emelee's dad or sister that she could find. Ms. Minnie went to Em's room and found a letter from Noel and a phonebook with Mokeith's number in it. She handed them to the detectives, and they told her to get her coat. They walked her to their car and took her to the morgue.

When the coroner pulled open the door and pulled out the slab holding Emelee Amil Maithers cold, stiff, and breathing no more, Ms. Minnie collapsed with grief. Detective Harford caught her in his arms and said, "Ms. Wells are you okay?" Ms. Minnie couldn't speak. She shook her head as she covered her mouth and sobbed.

Detectives Harford and Sams took Ms. Minnie back to her apartment. They gave her their cards and told her to call if she needed to anytime.

Detective Sams contacted Mokeith to tell him that Emelee had been murdered. Detective Harford contacted the Williams' household to inform them of Emelee's death. Mokeith, Ms. Minnie, and the Williams family gathered to say their final goodbye to Emelee.

After the funeral, Detectives Sams and Harford sat the family down to explain what happened to Emelee Amil Maithers. After class, Emelee was walking to her car alone when she was approached from behind and taken in the alley where she was brutally attacked by a person unknown to her.

Mokeith, the first to speak, asked, "Who did it?"

Reluctantly, Detectives Sams replied, "Deyon Winston is a known offender [he said while holding Deyon's mugshot]. We have a witness that places him on the scene at the time of the crime."

Ms. Minnie followed, "Do you have him? Is he in jail?"

Detective Sams replied, "No! We are actively looking for him, but no one has seen him since the assault." Noel cried. Her mom, dad, and siblings consoled her.

Mokeith asked, "Did they know each other? Why did he target her?"

Detective Harford answered, "No! They had no connection in life."

Ms. Minnie gave Noel Em's belongings. Noel and her family returned to Virginia with all that was left of Em, a bag full of memories and things. Ms.

Minnie went about life alone and lonely without Em. Mokeith was crushed by the death of his daughter, and he was outraged that the man who took her life roamed the streets freely.

Mokeith told everyone he was going back to Detroit, but he went underground, living in the streets of Chicago, looking for Deyon Winston. Mokeith found out that Deyon was hiding in an abandoned building. Mokeith followed him one night.

When Deyon was alone, Mokeith grabbed him and stabbed him so many times that every inch of his body was cut. Mokeith hid his body so well that no one found his body for weeks. Mokeith made it back to Detroit before the body was found.

Detectives Sams and Harford stopped by the diner where Ms. Minnie worked. They told her Deyon was murdered. Ms. Minnie felt sorrow for Em and the way she died, but she felt comforted in the thought that revenge came upon the one that slain Em. The case of Em's death was closed.

Ms. Minnie lived in Chicago alone until her dying day. Mokeith lived in the Metro-Detroit area. He worked in a factory. He got married and had more kids. He named his daughter Emelee to honor the daughter he didn't get a chance to raise.

In heaven, Emelee, Cecilia, Everett, and Marion reunited. Their souls found love and peace in heaven. Emelee was able to forgive Marian. The four of them vigilantly watched over Noel from heaven. They prayed for favor from God for Noel. Wanting the best for Noel is the one thread that continues to hold them together to this day.

CHAPTER 6

The Honey Bee Will Soar

Noel Ann Marie Williams, the valedictorian of her graduating class, was enjoying her last summer at home before going to college to study pediatric medicine.

Noel spent the summer after high school reading, working, and exercising. She wanted to enter college at the top of her game. Her sister went to an HBCU to study law school, and her brother made a career in the military, following in the footsteps of his father. Now, Noel was going to make her mark on the world.

One summer day, Noel received a huge package from Georgia. When she opened it up, she saw pictures of biological her mother and father. There was also letters and money in the box.

Her father's relatives wanted to reach out to her now that she was an adult in the hopes of having some type of relationship with her. She wrote them back and kept in contact with them. They asked if she could visit them in Georgia for their family reunion before she started college. Mr. and Mrs. Williams agreed to let her go to the reunion.

Noel had a blast meeting her birth father's family. They were so loving and friendly. She learned new details about her father. She realized her personality was very similar to her father's. Noel felt like this reunion was cathartic for her and her transition into adulthood.

Getting to know her father's family created a renewed bond between Noel and Everett. Every night before bed, she would look at pictures of her birth family and pray. She prayed for their happiness and salvation. She prayed for her new family. She prayed to God for continued grace for them all.

Driving home from work for the last time before leaving for college, Noel was elated by the possibilities of her future. Five minutes away from her house, Noel stopped at a red light.

When the light turned green, she proceeded through the intersection. She heard a voice from the vacant passenger seat say, "Hey, young girl!" Noel looked to see the young man from the dream she had years ago.

Out of the corner of her eye, she saw two angels sitting in the back seat. Their wings were spread throughout the car covering the body of each person in the car. Noel couldn't see anything as she felt an impact jolting her body in the seat. The loud sound of the collision, the metal scraping, and glass breaking scared Noel. Despite the intensity of the impact, Noel was not harmed.

Witnesses rushed over to Noel's car, confused that Noel was in the car alone. Witnesses searched and searched for the other three people thinking they flew out the window when the car crashed. When the police arrived, the witnesses told the police that there were four people in the car before it crashed. When the police talked to Noel, she swore she was alone in the car. Noel was shaking as the fear as she looked at the irreversible damage to her car. The driver that hit Noel was badly injured, but Noel. Noel thanked God for sparing her life.

Emergency vehicles quickly arrived on scene to take Noel and the other driver to the hospital. Michele and Vernon rushed to the hospital in a panic. As soon as Michele and Vernon reached the emergency room, doctors informed them that Noel received a thorough examination, and not one injury was found. Doctors and nurses called Noel "the blessing" and told her that God has something great in store for her.

First responders told the ER staff that He must've protected her during the crash. The man who ran the red light and hit Noel was in a coma with a head injury, a punctured lung, and ruptured spine. As thankful as Noel was to be healthy, she was heartbroken for the man fighting for his life.

That night, Noel tossed and turned until she fell asleep. There was a knock at the door. Her parents were deep in sleep, so Noel crept through the dark house and down the stairs to answer the door. Noel said, "Who is it?"

A deep, powerful voice answered, "God!"

Noel rushed to open the door. The entire world went pitch dark. Noel could see nothing, but the man completely covered in purple silk from her dream years old. It seemed like the man was ten feet tall and as solid as a brick wall. The man held a gold rod in one hand and a gold staff in the other.

Despite the dark and the silk covering, Noel can see the man looking at her. She says, "It is you! It's not safe out here at night, you should come inside."

He answers, "You should come outside!"

Noel says, "Let me get something to protect you!"

He replies, "You don't have to protect me. Come out! Trust me!"

Noel walks out the door. The man says, "I want to show you something. Come go with me!"

Noel was afraid to be outside in such darkness, but she put her hand in the man's hand. Noel says, "I'll go with you, but I need something to protect you. You don't know people; they are dangerous, especially in the night." The man exposed his neck. His skin was the color of pure 24-karat gold. He took his staff and pierced his neck, but nothing happened.

He said, "It's nothing that can harm me, and I have an army of angels that is never far from me." He snapped his fingers. Instantly, a male and a female angel appeared floating in a t formation. Noel looked in amazement.

He said, "It's never your job to protect me. Your job is to have faith."

Noel asked, "Faith? I don't have faith?"

He says, "From the moment I knocked on the door, you were filled with doubt. When it comes to your God, you should have no doubt. You should trust completely, have faith, and know that I know the way."

Noel felt bad; she said, "My God, I am so sorry. I didn't even realize what I was doing."

He said, "You are no longer a child, Noel! It's time to put childish thinking away. At all times, I need you clothed in faith. Wear it like it's your body armor as you fight in this war as my soldier. Noel, I have chosen you, and the time has come."

Noel says, "My Lord, I am ready to serve!"

The man said, "When people have doubt, they usually stumble. But, you, Noel, I won't let you stumble. You have a heart of gold. Dedicated! Innocent! Trustworthy! I know that I can trust you to tend to my flock, and you will care for the lest of thee as if you were caring for me."

Noel was moved by his words.

He added, "Wise! Though you were doubtful, you are wise to recognize danger. You are right about one thing; it is dangerous in the dark."

He snapped his fingers, and the earth was covered with light. Noel jumped up out of her sleep.

The End

www.ingramcontent.com/pod-product-compliance
Lightning Source LLC
Chambersburg PA
CBHW040547170726
48295CB00012B/622